The Bull Dancer

A Short Story of Sherlock Holmes

More by Dana Cameron

Fangborn Novels

Seven Kinds of Hell

Pack of Strays

Hellbender

**Emma Fielding Archaeology Mysteries
(now on Hallmark Movies & Mysteries)**

Site Unseen

Grave Consequences

Past Malice

A Fugitive Truth

More Bitter Than Death

Ashes and Bones

Also from DCLE:

Pandora's Orphans: A Fangborn Collection
Exit Interview: an a.k.a. Jayne novel
Anna Hoyt: A Novel of Colonial Crime

The Bull Dancer

A Short Story of Sherlock Holmes

Dana Cameron

The Bull Dancer:
A Short Story of Sherlock Holmes

DCLE Publishing LLC

ISBN-13: 978-1-7371536-6-5

The death of Sherlock Holmes hit me hard and left me grasping for meaning in a world that seemingly had abandoned all reason. Why had such a great man had gone, willingly, to meet one of the most diabolical foes he'd ever encountered? Without any plan or reinforcement? Without me? It was absurd. Why was he gone, with all of his talent and unparalleled mind, and I was left here, while *everyone else* was left here, made no sense.

I'd lost comrades before, but never a friend. *We* were *friends*. Brothers.

That selfish bastard.

I had long ago taken my grievances to the Almighty, who was, unsurprisingly, not forthcoming. My distress was acute and as a result, I was very dull. I couldn't bear to write the morally uplifting and heavily bowdlerized tales I sent to *The Strand Magazine*; these pale reflections of our raucous life seemed absurd to me now. I took a leave from my practice, and when my usual recourses—too much drinking, gambling, and brawling—did nothing to rouse me, I began looking for answers in the opposite direction of Heaven, that is to say, Whitehall.

As I've written often in my private notes, Mycroft

Holmes terrified me, as he would any sane, rational man. Nevertheless, I wrote to his office requesting an appointment, and that evening, received a telegram in reply. "SH dead and gone. I can do nothing for you. MH."

Not a word of our (presumably) shared grief or indication of his own loss, no willingness even to inquire on my purposes, only these bare ten words to dismiss me. Commiseration? I had not expected it, but this abrupt rejection of the hole in my world was cold even for the beast at the heart of the British government.

I returned to my practice. It was as simple as that: I had no use for suicides and if I was to occupy my time between drinking bouts, I might as well employ my medical skills meaningfully.

It was perhaps a month later that a lady, well-dressed in widow's weeds and heavily veiled, entered my waiting room. I am no Holmes, but I could tell at once she was young, wealthy, and, beneath her weeds, plump and slender in nearly the right proportions—though I profess to preferring a more solid fundament. Her card, expensive in its design, ink, and paper, read Mrs. Edmund Armstrong.

I introduced myself, asked her to sit, and inquired how I

might help.

"It is imperative I see Mr. Sherlock Holmes." She glanced around the room, as if expecting him to appear.

I couldn't imagine that anyone had not heard of his death, and began as gently as I could, well aware of my own acute distress on the subject. "You must have been out of the country, madam—"

"Indeed I have. He and I had an appointment to meet in Vienna. He would not be tardy, much less miss a meeting with *me*." She lifted her veil back, as if to demonstrate how foolish missing that appointment would be. Auburn brows, rather too thick, and a full mouth, with too much rouge.

She was pretty enough, in her way, but I was sad and bereft and angry. I could not repress a rude noise at the thought that Holmes would defy the grave for *her* over anyone else in the world, myself especially. "I am sorry to inform you, then, madam, that he is *dead*. He is no longer in a position to keep any appointment at all. This has been the case for three years now, and even the strictest arbiters of etiquette acknowledge the end of life as an acceptable excuse for missing a...missing a damned...assignation!"

Her look of shock could not have been more pronounced, and I immediately felt a rush of guilt, with redoubled anger that she'd caused me to utter such horrors. My emotions must have been plainly visible, because, for just an instant, I saw a twitch of her lips and an eyebrow raised in a familiar manner that was like a knife to my heart.

Not just a knife: the pain in my chest was beyond compare, as if a cannon ball had been shot into me at point-blank range. I couldn't catch my breath, my tongue thickened, and as much as I wanted, I could not close my eyes. A pain reminiscent of my old war wound shot through my left arm.

I hit the floor, and the woman rushed to my side, kneeling, and raising my head to her face. "You're not hurt, Watson? For God's sake, say that you are not hurt!"

The facial movements that so reminded me of him were now matched by the exact phrasing and emotions I knew so well in my deceased friend, Mr. Sherlock Holmes.

"Holmes?" I mumbled. My struggling brain attempted to reconcile what I saw, what I observed, and what I couldn't believe. Even with his talent for disguise... "How can it be?"

"A Holmes, but not your Holmes," she said. "And if you die, we'll both lose him forever!"

"But—"

"Damn it, Watson! If we can reach him in time, I can save him! And for that, I need you."

I was failing, my sight blurring and all reason leaving.

Despite the change of hair color and maquillage, I imagined that I was looking into the face of the woman I knew as the adventuress Irene Adler.

※

I awoke in my chair, confused, and every muscle aching. The hollowness in my chest spoke of an unremembered tragedy, momentarily at bay.

I saw that fair face, so calculating and cruel, now scrubbed of cosmetics and sans veil, observing me from the chair opposite. Holmes's chair.

"I don't know what you think you're doing, you wretch, but even if Holmes were alive, even if I did know his location, I would never reveal any of it to *you*. And what do you mean, not my Holmes?"

She hesitated, as if on the brink of a terrible admission. And the answer suggested itself to me, struck me, as hard as that cannon ball before.

"Dear God above! You are married to Holmes!"

Her face was a kaleidoscope of emotions, flickering as

quickly as a zoetrope.

"I always knew he'd been less than fully truthful in his description of his part in the scandal with the King of Bohemia," I continued bitterly. Suddenly, the hollow pain in my chest made sense: Holmes had secretly married, and had never trusted me enough to confide in me.

Not content with torturing me with her lies, the heartless creature burst into uproarious laughter. Again, I was reminded of his mannerisms.

"No, you dear idiot! Oh, this is priceless!" She laughed again. "Sherlock is my *brother*."

I attempted to sit up. "What? Impossible!"

"I'm not surprised," she said, dismissively. "You only discovered that he had a brother after several years of sharing rooms. Why wouldn't you suspect there were more of us?"

My mind boggled at the thought of a legion of Holmeses swooping around, laying waste to their home and the surrounding county with their chemical experiments, firearms practice, and martial arts. Holmes to me had always seemed a singularity, and I'd been stunned, and later horrified by the existence of Mycroft Holmes, a brutal genius of a man who worked behind the scenes on every aspect of the British Empire, and probably the Continent as well. "Are there? More of you?"

She tried, unsuccessfully, to smother a mocking grin. "You can hardly expect me to answer that, can you, when my brothers have been so closed-mouthed?"

"Then why come to me with this ridiculous announcement, so disguised? And why should I believe you? You are duplicity itself!"

"I only meant to observe you and the rooms you share with my brother to ascertain whether there was any update in his situation. But you recognized our family resemblance. And I would never have revealed myself, to you of all people, if it had not been of the utmost urgency: too many people know of your close connection and you would have been subject to interrogation if they suspected you knew...

"Holmes is not dead, as you and the rest of the world were meant to believe, but he is presently in mortal danger, and only we can save him."

She took the pulse at my wrist, with a firm, warm touch, as assured as if she were a trained nurse. "You seem well enough, though you have had a bad shock. I am sorry for that. But you must accompany me tomorrow. I have booked us tickets to Cambridge, and then a carriage to our destination from there."

"Why in the name of God should I believe any of this? Believe you?"

She hesitated, and then produced a small, hinged box. She opened it, and on one side was a much faded and creased daguerreotype showing two small children, a boy, about nine years old, and a girl of about eleven. The girl's hand was on the shoulder of the boy, and when I glanced at her, she nodded. Very carefully, I unfolded the image. Another child, possibly fifteen, was revealed to be unmistakably Mycroft Holmes. I reexamined the other children: the younger boy was Sherlock and the girl bore an uncanny resemblance to them both. On the back were the names: Mycroft, Sherlock, Merivale.

"It's hard to imagine either of them as children, isn't it? And yet, there we were."

I looked at her, and at the picture again. There was a real resemblance, but I still didn't trust my eyes or her.

Without me saying a word, she removed her glove, and I saw a faded, circular scar. A puncture wound. Looking again at the picture, I could see its match on the girl's hand.

Before I could stop myself, I took her hand to examine it closely. The scar was genuine.

"An early gift from Mycroft. You never knew what might set him off, or what he'd do if you thwarted him. If I couldn't placate him or avoid him, I learned to be quick and clever. I also learned at a young age that a photograph was invaluable proof in a world where even a king's word has no value."

My guest glanced at the brandy and gasogene; I helped myself, and with some reluctance, mixed a bandy and soda for her as well.

I was surprised at how much stronger I felt. Anger was a tonic, and the idea that Holmes might be alive was more restorative than a week by the seaside. As she packed a bag for me, I found myself listening to Irene Adler's—or should I say, Merivale Holmes's?—tale of what really happened with the Hereditary King of Bohemia.

"... I eventually learned that it would be far better to be queen of the stage than of any state, able to keep my freedom, my money, and the thrall over the audiences. And," she said with a little shrug, "certain individuals. Or rather, delighting in the experience of being enthralled oneself. When I met my future husband, I knew I could no longer play at love. I had to surrender to it.

"Once I realized simply leaving Willy—forgive me! I mean, when I realized that it was impossible to just leave His Majesty Wilhelm Gottsreich Sigismond von Ormstein, Grand Duke of Cassel-Felstein and hereditary King of Bohemia, I knew I had to take much more extensive action. Some gentlemen simply will not accept the fact that one's affections have been transferred to another."

"You mean Geoffrey?"

"Godfrey, Mr. Godfrey Norton, Doctor Watson. The king is not fit to wipe Godfrey's boots, and my husband proves that a thousand times a day, both in his affection for me, and in the way he conducts his professional business."

"Surely it would have been easy enough for you to request the assistance of your eldest brother to smooth over the international issues," I said. Even thinking of him left a coppery taste in my mouth.

Some of my distaste must have showed, because Merivale Holmes became grave. "You've met Mycroft?"

"Yes."

"You find him an affable sort of gentleman? The soul of kindness and empathy?"

I recalled his cold, bloodless telegram. "No, I'm sorry to say I do not."

"I know that you and Sherlock are in occasional contact with him, when he needs someone less indolent to find something useful for him. I imagine you've seen his temper and his monstrous physical power, which is the equal of his awesome intellect. Thus, imagine what it was like growing up with him, refusing to behave as he wished."

I knew that Holmes the younger had developed his unorthodox fighting style as a youth precisely to deal with a larger, stronger, angrier opponent. I looked at the dainty creature sitting across from me and though I knew she had a will of steel and the resolution of a man, I hated the thought of Mycroft Holmes's rage turned against her.

"Singing was—is—my gift. As a girl, when I sang, Mycroft was calm, and my voice was the only thing capable of easing his persistent headaches. But when I insisted on refusing the hand of every pimply-faced squire's son he put in front of me, he became violent. Threatened to lock me up.

"I determined to find my way in the world by my wits and my other talents rather than to live confined in my rooms. I escaped to America—that is another story—but my very name still makes Mycroft livid, which is why I had to go to such lengths to have Sherlock free me from the king of Bohemia and attend my wedding. His presence would ensure that the king was satisfied I was done with him forever. I had to do it all without Mycroft discovering me.

"We had to make it crystal clear to the world that Sherlock Holmes had witnessed my escape, even though it meant appearing as if he'd been outsmarted by a woman—much less an opera singer, a demimonde. To be fair, most of it was my idea, but I let him think that it had been inspired by his own theatrical impulses—how much more romantic if I thwart the evil king and escape with the man I love? Sherlock was more than willing; his own opinion of Willy was very low."

I wasn't convinced. "He never told me. I never noticed him contriving any of these plans you mention. You are taking advantage of me."

"That guinea on his waistcoat pocket? A gift from Godfrey to his best man."

"I was there. I saw...nearly...everything. I saw...nothing of what you claim."

"You saw precisely what you were meant to, you were told what we needed to convey. All that nonsense about the rush to the church and the need for witnesses? Legal rubbish, of course! Godfrey and I had to catch our steamer to Calais, that's all. I had thought I wanted a king—after all, Mycroft has the ear of a certain gracious lady and Sherlock is fast becoming indispensable to her—but...power without purpose is an unworthy goal. Once I realized I could do better, I devised the plan to extricate myself."

I allowed myself a gasp at the audacity of it all: Seducing a king, and then having the gall to imagine he wasn't enough? The woman was outrageous. And yet, there was wisdom in her words about power and purpose.

"I fled him, yes, taking the cabinet photograph as insurance. But that theft, despite my promises to him of its real purpose—my protection—spurred him into action. Poor Willy couldn't take it in that I was leaving him for good; it was quite something to see, like a fat schnauzer, asleep by the fire, who is suddenly alerted to the presence of a rabbit outside and thinks himself half his actual age. It was comical, startling, and distressing all at once. I didn't wish the poor idiot dead from a heart attack, but neither was I expecting such an active expression of his ire...

"When he approached Sherlock, I realized that I had to

surrender the photo for him to leave me alone. But I wanted to spite him, for his many instances of violence against me and my property." She shuddered delicately. "I'd fought off his men more than once, always fleeing, always hiding. That's no life for anyone, even an 'adventuress,' to live. I hoped I might elude him, and Godfrey and I could marry in peace; when he made me postpone our hopes, Willy had to pay for that, and at a rate that even he would notice. More than that, he had to be utterly convinced that, short of my death, he was completely free of me and any claim on him. He had to be convinced that his kingdom and his 'brilliant match' with Norway's princess was going forward, unsullied by scandal. He needed... *theater*."

"Why did Holmes not confide in me? I might have assisted him—you both!"

"We needed you as a witness. You are sea-green incorruptible, Watson, and if you believed it, so would the world. You had to relate what we *needed* to be the truth. Plus, there was the matter of your fictional publications in *The Strand*..."

I shook my head. "No. Holmes and I have trusted each other with mortal secrets before. He knows I'm to be relied upon."

"Who is the person you fear most in the world? What if you had to risk the dangerous wrath of that person, in order to save one unbelievably dear to you? Could you do it?"

I suddenly understood: Mycroft Holmes again.

Dark anger flickered behind her eyes. I understood that she detested Mycroft as much as I did, and probably with greater reason. "Mycroft could look at you, as I did, and see at an instant that you were lying. You had to be convinced of what you'd seen.

"Sherlock has been poisoned by a Mr. Jeremiah Baldwin. Although Baldwin appears to be no more than a well-respected researcher and scientist, holding many patents for new drugs, he is the... poisoner of choice for criminals around the world. Sherlock was on his trail when Baldwin had him poisoned—partly in revenge for an old hurt my brother had done him, partly as a demonstration of his new poison. There's only one antidote, a compound of the austral trefoil plant, *Lotus australis* to be precise, found only in Australia. Sherlock has summoned me to help him, but I have to do this without alerting Mycroft to my presence in England." She shuddered. "He'd have me committed to an insane asylum if he caught me."

Dana Cameron 21

"And?"

"In order to make the antidote we need the *Lotus australis*. Baldwin's greenhouse is a marvel, the toast of the academic world. His home is like a fortress—because of the interest he holds for those criminals and because his research in biological weapons of war. Fortunately for us, he has a weakness for music."

I would never have believed any of this, if I'd believed it was "Irene Adler" telling me. But Merivale or whatever her name—her face and mannerisms so reminded me of Holmes that I felt my throat tighten whenever I looked at her. The mere idea that Holmes himself might be alive was enough to spur me to action. And if—no, when!—we did save his life, I'd put my boot up his arse for the grief he'd subjected me to.

I cleared my throat. "And my part?"

"I am the distraction. You'll acquire what's needed, and deliver it to my brother."

"It is possible I'll be recognized."

"You needn't be concerned. I'll be masked—everyone knows I've 'retired' from the stage, so it was a condition of our agreement, as was finding an excellent pianist to accompany me. Everyone in attendance, most of whom will be poison merchants and drug merchants, will also be masked. You see, I've thought of everything."

✳

After the late night and its revelations, I slept well past my usual hour. I only roused when heard the door to my chamber open, and the soft tread of a woman's foot scraped the floor. Mrs. Norton—I had determined that was her preferred name now—stood there, regarding me with an unreadable gaze. She clutched a large bundle, wrapped in a cloak, with her left hand. In her right, was a wicked-looking straight razor.

My fingers were already closing around the grip of my pistol, when she unceremoniously dumped the bundle on the table, two steps brought her over to the wash stand, and she placed the razor upon it. She glanced in the ewer and nodded.

"Good, you're awake. We have much to do today, and you'll want to wash first. You may leave your pistol where it is for the moment, Doctor. We'll need it later, no doubt. I'll be similarly armed."

I glanced at the bundle of black on the table, and observed a pair of lady's boots, but in a size large enough for a gentleman. I understood her intent.

"No. It's impossible. I cannot—"

"I need an accomplice. I was forced to leave Miss McCune-Smith, my assistant and medical advisor, behind, when she fell prey to pneumonia. I must now rely on you—Mr. Norton is a man of many talents, but medicine is not one of them. There's no one else. An older woman will be more forgettable than a gentleman, in any case. The mustache goes."

I sputtered. "The audacity—"

"Come now, it will take only two or three weeks for it to grow back properly, if you decide to. I personally think you are even more handsome without it."

"But if I am masked...?"

"We may need every second. No mask would fully conceal a mustache, and if the mask should fall, it would give everything away instantly. The mustache goes."

Her eyes softened. "I know that you are an admirer of my sex, and no doubt have studied the gait and movements of ladies... in the course of your medical practice! I've no doubt you'll make a fine attendant matron. And I've modified our garments somewhat to suit our needs."

She shut the door behind her, and I released a shuddering breath, my heart pounding like cannon fire. As much as I wanted to trust her, and as much as she claimed to need me, she was too dangerous to take for granted. An adventuress, who had so little regard for the social principles that made an Empire—and a Holmes on top of it all? But on the remotest chance that Sherlock Holmes was still alive, I would do that and so much more.

*

During our journey, Mrs. Norton distracted me from the discomfort of my new garments with the details of her plan. Having performed for Mr. Baldwin before, she knew the layout of the house and how it was protected.

Some miles outside of Cambridge, a magnificent home was lit by torchlight. The clouds, wind, and rain gave the place an eerie look, made even more sinister by the ghostly glass structure visible behind the house. Armed men could be seen at intervals, guarding a small crowd of thirty or so select villains, scientists, and manufacturers. As Mrs. Norton had promised, they were all masked, but still, I feared my disguise would be revealed at every moment; although I had performed women's roles in boarding school theatricals, it had never been in heels. But as Mrs. Norton had said, no one paid any heed to a tottery old lady. I was of no importance.

A moment after our introduction, Mrs. Norton spoke to the lady of the house, indicating that her companion—me—had suffered from the chill and difficult roads. I was whisked away to a drawing room and promised calm and quiet.

Once the door closed and I was left to my tea, I took a candle and immediately made my way to the door to the library. It was empty, fortunately for me. Two glass doors fitted in between the bookcases on the far wall, and I knew these led to the conservatory. I could feel the change in the temperature of the room as I approached, and when I opened the doors, a waft of warm, humid air, redolent of smells of growing things, greenery, and the heavy scent of exotic flowers washed over me. I closed the door hastily behind me. I moved quickly as I could, but the confounded skirts sought to trip me up at almost every step.

Sweat poured down my face, as I neared the center part of the building. Mrs. Norton had informed me that the plant I sought would be at the warmest spot in the room. I was reminded unpleasantly of my time in Asia, which brought an unexpected desire to leave this place, post haste. Panic welled in my chest, and I'm ashamed to say that without the notion of Sherlock Holmes being alive I might have fled. As it was, it took every bit of my concentration to breathe normally and proceed with my plan.

I found the location and disaster: Mrs. Norton had not known that there was another small glass room within the green house, and, dammit all, locked. I shook the door again, hoping that it was only stuck, but nothing about the house suggested anything but efficiency, security, and attention to detail.

Even with the condensation rolling down the windows, I could see within the pretty pinkish flowers of the blooming shrub that matched exactly the drawing she'd given me. The precautions surrounding it were further proof of its rarity and value. A small table with a notebook, dissection tools, and packets—probably of harvested seeds—sat next to a pot with the deadly plant itself. I cursed. I couldn't risk breaking the glass. I had to remove my gloves, with difficulty, and spend valuable time picking the lock.

Finally. The lock released.

I unbuttoned the back panel of my skirts. Concealed at my backside, instead of a bustle, was a small cloth bundle of waxed cotton lined with remnants of a heavy quilt. It unfolded into a bag, in which I put the plant itself, along with the notebook and seed packets. No longer in its protected room, it would still be insulated from the cold and wind of a blustery British October. I closed the door carefully behind me.

A door opened, and I extinguished my candle.

"Mrs. Johnson, what are you doing out—? You must stay away from that!"

I can only imagine what the maid saw: a stout old woman wandering, fumbling at a locked door, dazed by this tropical heat.

I pretended to ignore her, and hastened away, stumbling across a fallen palm branch. I had been in the military only a short time, but under such circumstances as to have had the opportunity to hear men in extremes of anger, fear, and duress. The language I acquired from them—colorful and vitriolic—spilled from my lips, in my accustomed voice. It may have raised the temperature in the stifling greenhouse by a few degrees.

The maid screamed. I swore again, and gave up at pretense, running for the door to the outside, the potted plant wrapped and snug under my arm like a rugby ball.

I glanced at my watch: the recital would soon be over, and I was still trapped at the back of the building. I had to get outside—

Catastrophe. The maid's screams brought the guards to the outside door of the conservatory. They unlocked the door, barring my own way out. I cast about, and saw the stairs to the mezzanine that offered a view of the upper branches of the trees and vines. I fled upstairs, away from the ground floor doors and easier means of egress.

The staircase was wide and splendid, and the guards spotted me. Five against one were hardly fair odds. I felt my nerves melt away, and a quiet stole over me. Time slowed, and I surveyed my options: shooting would draw more attention and my chances of hitting them all and stopping them were not good in this gloomy light. I could not brawl with them and protect my precious bundle at the same time.

Like a puffer fish, I decided to bluster and threaten, creating a sense of greater danger than I was.

"Stop right there!" I was pleased at the note of soldierly command in my voice. I raised the pistol toward the roof of the greenhouse. "One more step, and the apple of your master's eye and the heart of his chemical empire is destroyed! Think of his fury when he knows that you were responsible!"

They paused, exchanging glances. I could hear a crystalline note rang out in the distance—"Stride la vampa" from *Il Trovatore*—and I savored that moment of balancing on the precipice of action and inaction, violence and art.

Silence: the song had ended. Applause erupted, breaking my spell. A guard stepped forward.

I shot three times, shattering the glass of the ceiling.

Shards rained down, vitreous daggers, and the structure creaked, shifting under the belting wind. Men's screams followed me as I hiked up my skirts and dashed into the main part of the first floor, running as quickly as I could to the front of the house.

I heard a cry of "fire!" and through the windows, saw masked guests below screaming in panic, running from the house for their waiting carriages.

At the side of the house, away from the fleeing guests, a weird scene presented itself. Two masked figures, one as slight and lithe as an angel and the other as massive and monstrous as Leviathan, were engaged in a bizarre dance. The angel's quicksilver movements reminded me of the paintings on the ruins of the island of Crete, athletic youth vaulting over the bulls, braving death itself with fearless grace. If I had not formerly witnessed Sherlock Holmes's unique brand of hand to hand combat—indirect, ungentlemanly, and brutal—with its darting moves and sneaking strikes—I would not have understood the scene before me.

If Merivale had taught Sherlock how to act, then Sherlock had taught Merivale how to fight, using the technique he'd developed specifically for combating their brother Mycroft.

Mrs. Norton was wearing a garment similar in design to the one she'd given me. She had at some point removed her skirts and bustle, revealing a narrow pair of trousers. She unfurled the material of the skirt, whirling it over her head like a banner and snapping the end at Mycroft like a whip, keeping him at bay. With her increased range of movement, she now entangled Mr. Holmes's hands. With a tremendous bellow of frustration, he pulled against the fabric, yanking it from her hands, but she gained a few seconds as he untangled himself, delivering three lightning punches to his side. Even with the mask on, her entire being radiated diabolical glee.

I watched transfixed as she danced in and out of his reach, a jab here, a sly kick there, which served only to enrage the giant man. I feared that if he caught her, he would rip her limbs from her body or bludgeon her to death with his mallet-like fists.

I descended the stairs to the ground floor, opened a door, and raised my pistol. I could not let her be destroyed: she had risked all to save her brother, my dearest friend.

I hesitated: vile as he may be, Mycroft *was* crucial to the functioning of the British government. Shooting him, no matter the cause, would leave a gaping hole in the state I'd sworn to protect. Murder, it would be, but infinitely worse to me, perhaps also treason.

In the moment I paused, a new kind of frightfulness emerged. A wagon tore down the drive to the house. A child, barely large enough to have climbed to the box much less command the pair of horses, reined them to a halt. A tall, gaunt specter emerged from the inside, unsteadily, his gaze fixed on the house. More children, larger than the driver, also emerged. They surrounded the man, armed with clubs and knives. The entire party might have been the study for a painted allegory of famine and war.

"Enough, Mycroft. She's only here at my request, and you know well she understood the risk involved." His voice was weak, but the tone and cadence told me it was my friend, Sherlock Holmes. My heart cracked to see him so haggard; but at the same time, it leapt to see him alive. "Is it too much to assume that you might be here for a similar reason?"

It was. Mycroft bellowed, "The pair of you made fools of me! Again!"

"No one knows that, Mycroft," Merivale said. "You have only to ignore this: everyone was masked, there was an inferno and chaos. No one needs know a thing." She had taken advantage of the distraction and now her pistol was out and pointed at him.

The gargantuan man did not move, and I understood: all three of *them* would know. I watched the triangle of siblings, each glaring at the other, poised to act at the brink of death and dishonor. I raised my pistol again.

Finally, Mycroft held up a hand and his carriage appeared. He vanished inside, and the driver whipped the horses into a gallop.

The spell broken, I realized that I'd been holding my breath. Inhaling deeply, I coughed: the fire was growing worse. I ran out of the building as a team drawing a water pump pulled around to the front of the burning house.

✻

The less said about the rest of that awful night, the better. The flight to the nearby farmhouse where Mr. Holmes the younger had been staying with his small army of homeless children. The shouting and chaos only resolved when I barked out orders: I told Mrs. Norton to leave the medical decisions to me, informed the Baker Street Irregulars that there was nothing to be gained by standing guard over Holmes while his two closest friends worked to save him, and demanded that Sherlock himself should save his breath for staying alive long enough for me to administer the antidote. Mrs. Norton nodded and bundled the urchins away while my long-lost friend nodded weakly, fading. I focused on my ministrations and tried to ignore that the acclaimed diva of the Imperial Opera of Warsaw distracted the children by instructing them how best to loot a burning building for the most portable and salable treasures safely.

She returned on their leave, standing nearby as I ground the dried black seeds of the austral trefoil, glancing occasionally at the note book I'd stolen from the greenhouse.

"Did you know Mycroft would be there?" I added a very small amount of the ground seeds to the liquid medium.

She shook her head quickly, and I realized she was now recovering from the shock of the evening's events. "No. Apparently he has business with Baldwin in his professional capacity, as I might have anticipated. Mycroft arrived late, while I was singing Schubert's 'Ständchen.' When I recognized him, I altered the tone of my voice for the next piece. But he recognized me; I changed it back, and sang Azucena's aria, my most famous piece. I'd hoped that final note might carry, to alert you. Apparently, one of the Irregulars spying upon the house alerted Sherlock to my presence. Sherlock hoped to take advantage of the distraction and help steal the plant himself."

"And now there will be rumors of a mysterious soprano whose clarity of tone shattered a greenhouse." I filled the syringe. "You started the fire?"

"I didn't have to. With the noise of the shots and the ruin of the greenhouse, the audience panicked. Someone knocked over a candelabra." She smiled with the kind of vanity I recognized in her younger brother. "But I *did* bring down the house."

Holmes was no longer conscious; tremors began to wrack his wasted body. Both of us stared at the syringe. I took a breath and plunged the needle into my friend's arm.

Nothing happened.

His face went blue: Sherlock Holmes was no longer breathing.

That miserable bastard had convinced me he was dead for three years, only to die right before my eyes while I tried to revive him.

Anger and despair filled me. I slapped him, hard as I could. Once, twice, and again.

I administered a large dose of stimulant, all too aware of his tolerance, hoping that I wasn't actively killing him myself.

Mrs. Norton pinched his hand. "Damn it, Sherlock! You wake up, or you'll be sorry!" Her voice held none of its usual authority, evoking the memory of a childhood plea. A moment passed, still and heavy as we watched.

Holmes stirred, and coughed; rolling over, he vomited on my shoes and skirts. Wiping his mouth, he struggled to sit up; we hastened to assist him.

"Merivale, you're here." He sounded like an approximation of his old self, though his voice was hoarse.

"Of course." She replied, now as composed as if she'd come back from a walk on a spring day.

"Watson, we have a great deal to discuss." He identified me easily, despite the remnants of my female costume, my clean-shaven face, and mask.

I could not control the quaver in my voice. I sniffed, and

wiped my eyes with my smoke-scented handkerchief; it came away smudged with makeup.

"We do indeed, Holmes."

*

Acknowledgments

I owe many thanks to:

- ❖ My Sherlockian friends who suggested the music I used in the story.
- ❖ My beta readers, Charlaine Harris, Toni L.P. Kelner, and John Goodrich.
- ❖ Diana Gill, who did the copy editing.
- ❖ James Goodwin, for everything, always.

Dana Cameron writes across many genres, but especially crime and speculative fiction. Her work, inspired by her career in archaeology, has won multiple Anthony, Agatha, and Macavity Awards, and her short story "Femme Sole" was short-listed for the Edgar Award. Dana is best known for the Emma Fielding archaeology mysteries (now on Hallmark Movies & Mysteries) and the Fangborn urban fantasy novels. When she isn't traveling or visiting museums, she spends her time weaving, spinning, and yelling at the TV about historical inaccuracies. You can find out more about Dana and her writing on her author website and blog at danacameron.com.